Through the Night

written by Jim Aylesworth

illustrated by Pamela Patrick

ATHENEUM BOOKS FOR YOUNG READERS

Atheneum Books for Young Readers
An imprint of Simon & Schuster Children's Publishing Division
1230 Avenue of the Americas
New York, New York 10020

Book design by Angela Carlino

The text of this book is set in Graham.
The illustrations are rendered in pastel.

First Edition

Printed in Hong Kong by South China Printing Co. (1988) Ltd.
10 9 8 7 6 5 4 3 2 1

Library of Congress Cataloging-in-Publication Data
Aylesworth, Jim.
Through the night / by Jim Aylesworth; illustrated by Pamela Patrick.—1st ed.
p.   cm.
Summary: Daddy drives through the night, thinking of his wife and children,
who greet him upon his arrival home.
ISBN 0-689-80642-6
[1. Night—Fiction. 2. Fathers—Fiction.] I. Patrick, Pamela, ill. II. Title.
PZ7.A983 Th   1998
[E]—dc21
97-7281
CIP   AC

For those who wait,

. . . with love!

—J. A.

Dedicated to my children, Jennifer, Brandon and Lisa.

Thank you M. M.

—P. P.

As the moon slowly rose
from behind a line of distant trees,
a car sped north along the highway.

Passing mile after mile of
fence and rolling fields, the lonely
driver thought of home
. . . his children
. . . his wife.

Music played softly on the radio.
The engine gave a muffled roar.
And the wind wuffled at the edge of the window.

Ahead, the lanes were dotted

with moving lights

. . . red taillights rushing

to the city and beyond

. . . white headlights

coming, coming, always larger and larger

. . . moving lights

. . . cars and trucks all

passing in the early night.

Gradually, mile after mile, moonlit fields began
to meld with the fringes of the city.

And gradually, more and more
lights sparkled the passing scene
. . . billboards
. . . gas stations
. . . motels
. . . water towers and tall
antennas topped with blinking red.

Factories rose—dark silhouettes
against the sky.
Pale windows reflected the moonlit clouds,
and smokestacks streamed into the night.

And all the while, mile after mile,
the music played, the engine roared, the
wind wuffled at the edge of the window,
and the lonely driver thought of home
. . . his children
. . . his wife.

Rising, the highway spanned a
glittering river.

And seen from the top of the
bridge's sweeping arc, the city
cast a reddish glow against the sky.

Mile after mile . . .

Mile after mile . . .

. . . more and more cars

. . . more and more trucks.

And all around at every side,
countless lights sparkled the night.

Ahead, the city buildings gleamed
like boxes draped in diamonds.

As the car sped nearer,
the skyline seemed to grow
taller until the buildings
nearly filled the sky.

And all the while, mile after mile,
the lonely driver thought of home
. . . his children
. . . his wife.

Gradually, the lanes curved broadly
and slipped among the other lanes
passing above and below.

Then up a gently rising ramp.
Then around, and up,
and down again.

With the turning, the tall buildings of the city fell
behind, and the car was headed west on
a street frantic with neon light.

And for block after block, the
colors flashed.

GAS FOR LESS   LAUNDROMAT

PHARMACY   CARRY-OUT

BARBER SHOP   CLEARANCE SALE

REAL ESTATE   BURGER PLACE

Then, almost knowingly, the car turned
left onto a quiet street.

Houses nestled snugly side by side.
Street lamps made leafy shadows
on the lawns.

A turn to the right, up a
hill, and past a darkened school,
and then a park with empty swings.
And on . . .

. . . until, at last, the car slowed, turned into a drive, and came to a stop.

The driver turned off the motor, took his suitcase from the seat, and hurried up the walk.

As he reached the steps, the door opened, and two children dressed in pajamas came running across the porch.

"Daddy!" they called.

"Well, well, well!" said their dad,
as he put the suitcase down and lifted
the children into his arms.
"I was afraid that you'd be in bed
by now."

"Mom said we could wait up to say
good night," said the girl.
"I'm sure glad she did!" said their
dad. "I missed you."
Then he set them down, picked up
the suitcase, and, together at last, they
went inside.

"Well, well, well!" said their dad,
as he put the suitcase down and lifted
the children into his arms.
"I was afraid that you'd be in bed
by now."

"Mom said we could wait up to say
good night," said the girl.
"I'm sure glad she did!" said their
dad. "I missed you."
Then he set them down, picked up
the suitcase, and, together at last, they
went inside.

While, in the driveway, the car sat as
still as the night, with the moon mirrored
in its glass.

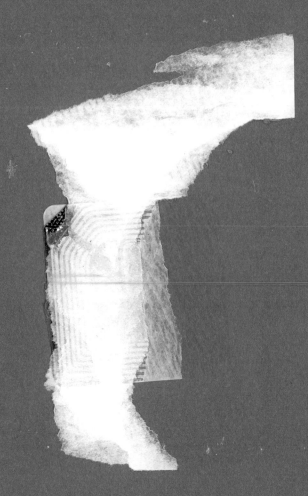